Dedicated to everyone who dreams of doing the most amazing job on earth, nursing.

A POST HILL PRESS BOOK
ISBN: 978-1-63758-443-9
ISBN (eBook): 978-1-63758-550-4

I Want to Be A NURSE When I Grow Up
© 2022 by Nurse Blake
Created in collaboration with Timmy Bauer
All Rights Reserved

Post Hill Press
New York • Nashville
posthillpress.com

Published in the United States of America
Distributed by Simon & Schuster
1 2 3 4 5 6 7 8 9 10

I Want to Be a NURSE When I Grow Up

NURSE BLAKE

TIMMY BAUER

Blake was watching his ALL TIME favorite show.

A MEDICAL DRAMA called:

"NURSE MAL PRACTICE"

Hey, **Nurse Mal**, you're **not** this patient's nurse!
He's a loner. He doesn't go by the book.

"I **want** to be just like | **NURSE MAL**."

"Even the **BUTT** chin."

"Class, **today** we're taking a field trip to the **HOSPITAL**!"

"**You're** going to find out what it's like to be a **NURSE**."

Who do you think was the first one off the bus?

That was amazing!
But Blake was not prepared for what he saw next...
The struggles of nursing. The next nurses he met were...

RED EYES

TIRED BACK

Stinky Pits

GROSS COFFEE

The Fourteen-hour-night-shift NURSE

The Grossed-out NURSE

Who stole my pen?
Where is the bladder scanner?
I need help in bed six now!
YELLING
Veins popping out of head
Clenched fists...
...of rage
The Cranky NURSE

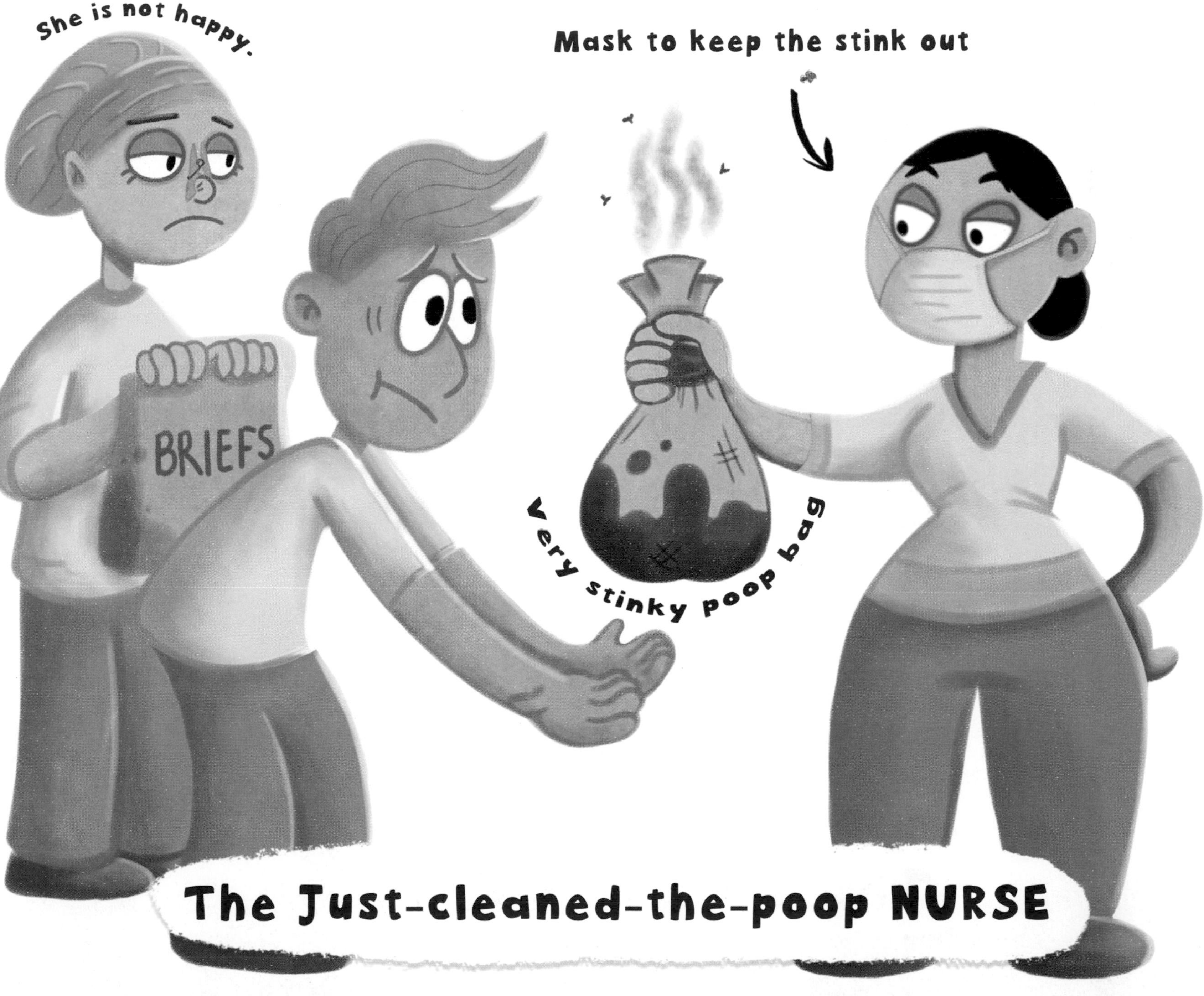

The Just-cleaned-the-poop NURSE

Some of these nurses didn't seem at all like the ones on TV.

THE JUST-CLEANED-THE-POOP NURSE

Blake was confused.

He thought nursing was going to be his job as a grown-up.

But it was not like what he thought.

He was so sad. He couldn't watch his favorite show.

How could the TV be so wrong?

Blake didn't know if he wanted to be a nurse anymore.

He was so sad. He couldn't focus in class.

He was so sad. He couldn't eat ice cream on ICE CREAM DAY!

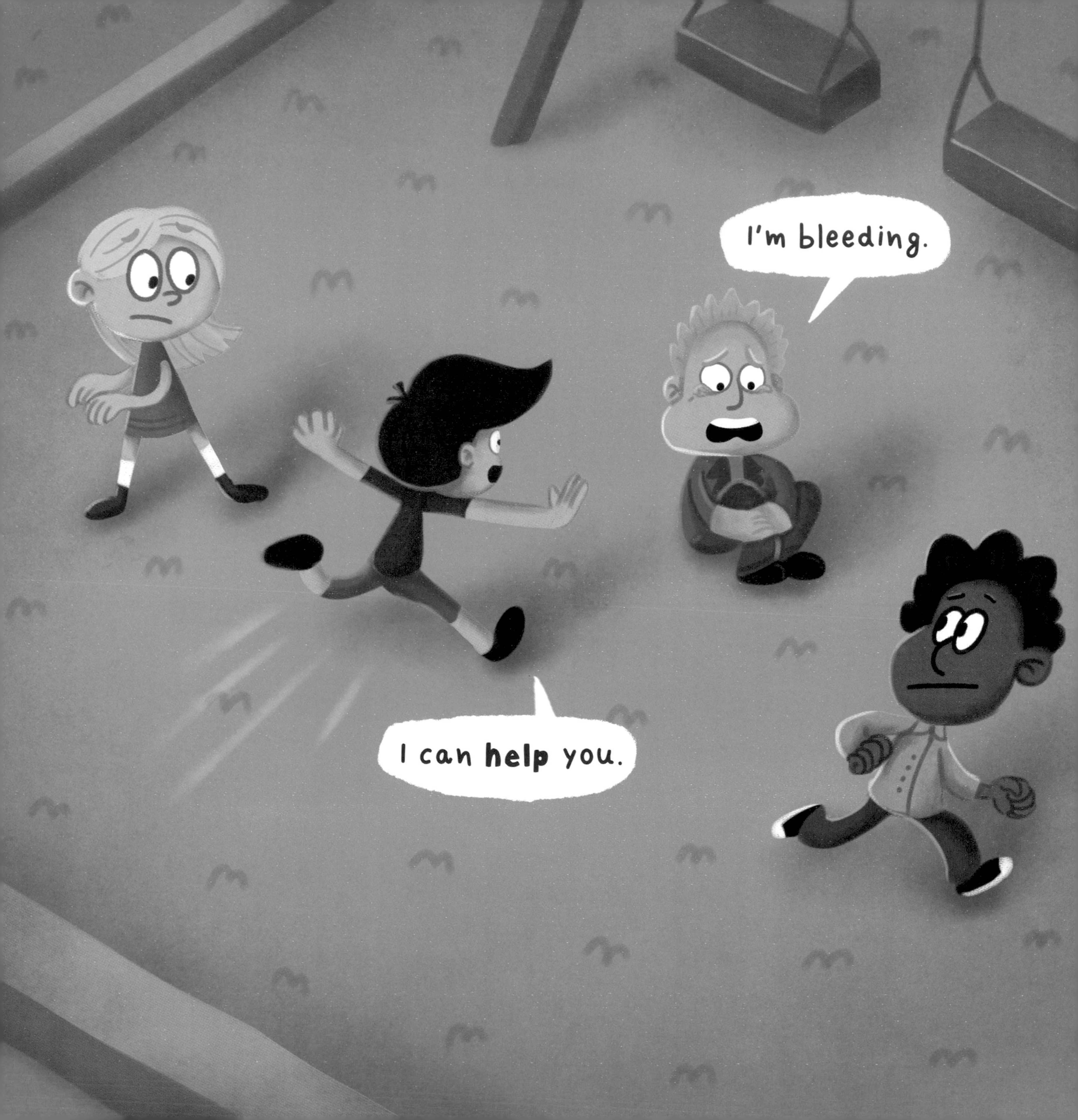
I'm bleeding.
I can **help** you.

You **dropped** the toy, Matt!
You call that a **SAFE SCENE**??
Lives are at stake here!

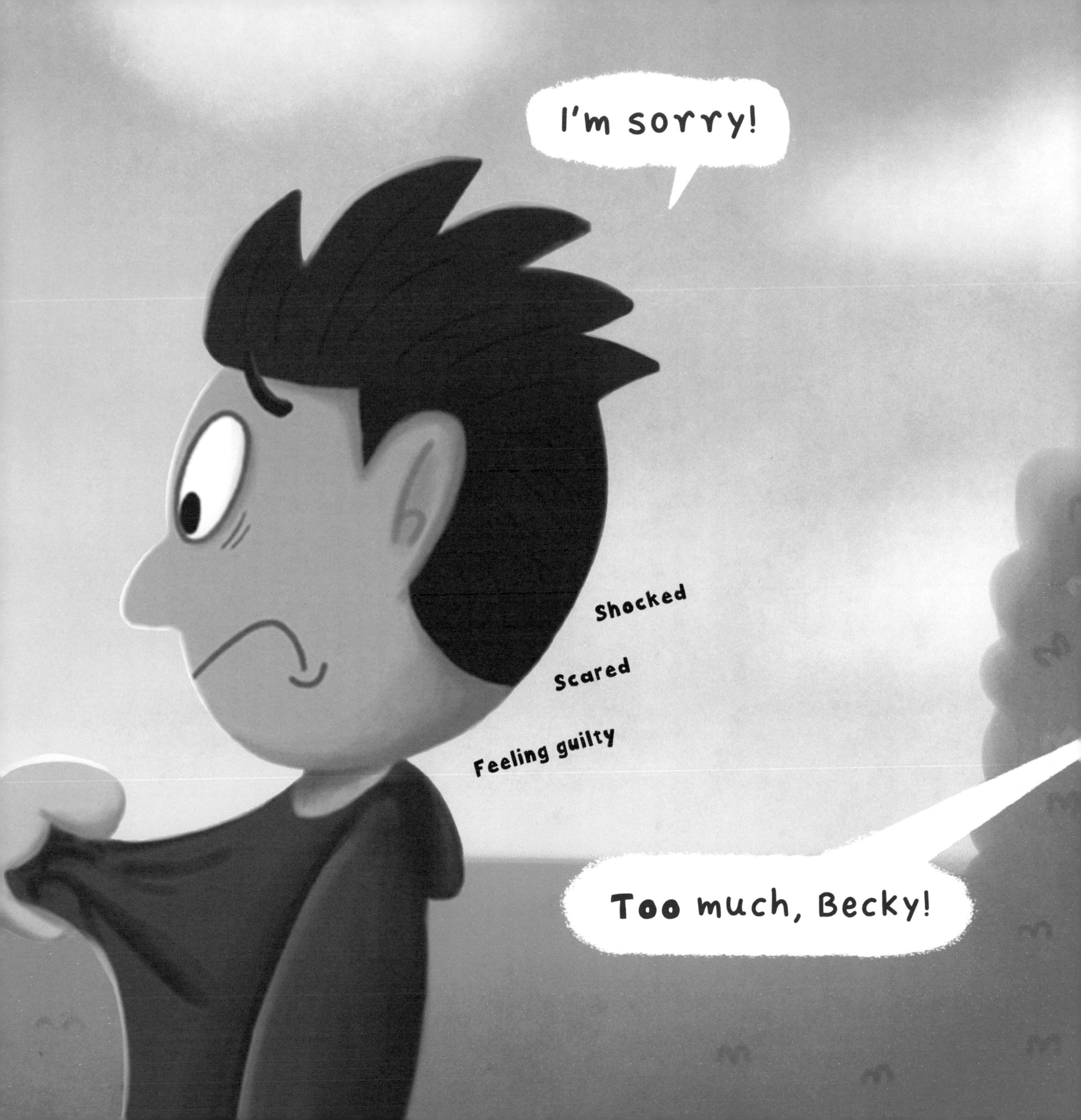
I'm sorry!
Shocked
Scared
Feeling guilty
Too much, Becky!

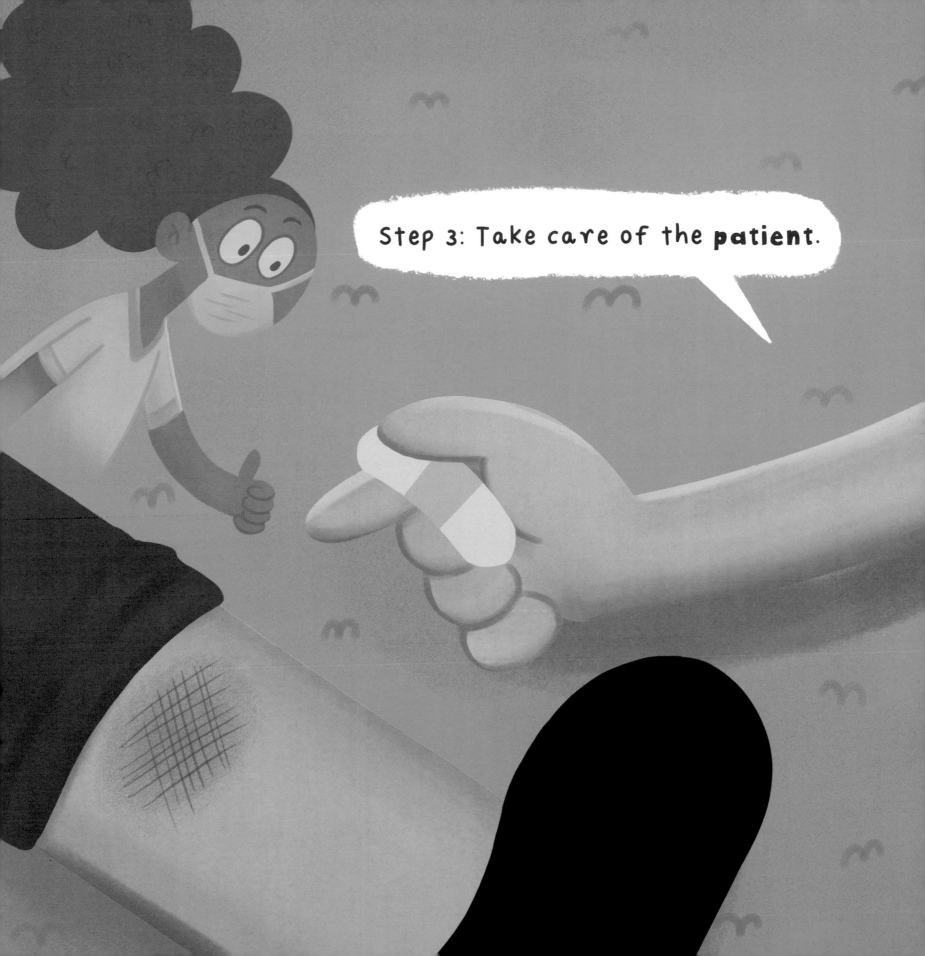

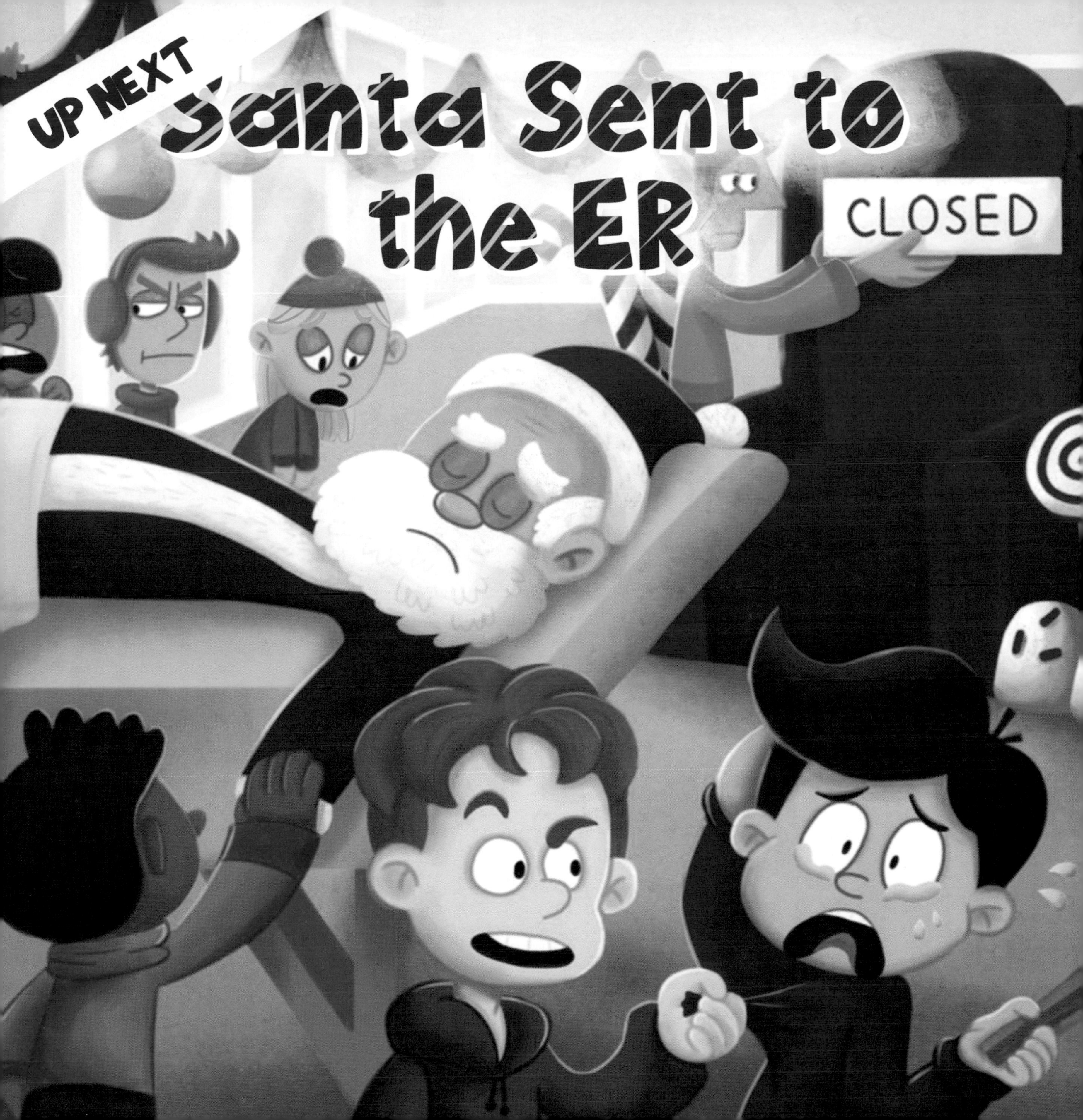
UP NEXT
Santa Sent to the ER
CLOSED